Bee awakened to Jacky standing over her. . . .

It was his presence, more than any sound, that woke her. And she did not startle as she had when he leaned over her by the sliding screen door. Now, in her dark bedroom, and just as she came up out of sleep, his being there felt deeply familiar.

He lay across her, over the sheet. Bee waited for him to say what he was supposed to: You're hurt. Don't move. I'll get you out of this. *He said nothing, and his body was heavy on top of hers, much heavier than it had been in the woods.*

"I can't move my legs," she whispered. Was that true? It was what she had always said. . . .

"Brilliantly written. . . . This is neither an easy book to read nor does it suggest any neat resolutions. What Coman does offer, masterfully, is honesty, compassion, and even a glimmer of hope."

—*School Library Journal*

OTHER PUFFIN BOOKS YOU MAY ENJOY

Dancing on the Edge Han Nolan

Edge Michael Cadnum

I Never Asked You to Understand Me Barthe DeClements

Tell Me Everything Carolyn Coman

What Jamie Saw Carolyn Coman

Zero at the Bone Michael Cadnum

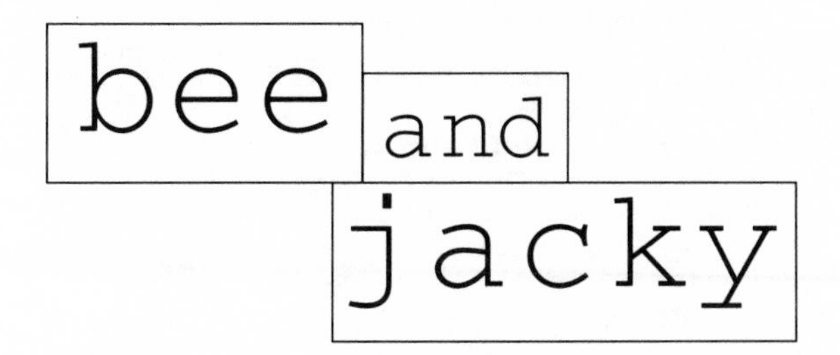

Carolyn Coman

for Sheri —
Welcome to the Program!
love, Carolyn

PUFFIN BOOKS

PUFFIN BOOKS
Published by the Penguin Group
Penguin Putnam Books for Young Readers,
345 Hudson Street, New York, New York 10014, U.S.A.
Penguin Books Ltd, 27 Wrights Lane, London W8 5TZ, England
Penguin Books Australia Ltd, Ringwood, Victoria, Australia
Penguin Books Canada Ltd, 10 Alcorn Avenue,
Toronto, Ontario, Canada M4V 3B2
Penguin Books (N.Z.) Ltd, 182-190 Wairau Road,
Auckland 10, New Zealand

Penguin Books Ltd, Registered Offices:
Harmondsworth, Middlesex, England

First published in the United States of America
by Front Street Books, 1998
Published by Puffin Books,
a member of Penguin Putnam Books for Young Readers, 1999

10 9 8 7 6 5 4 3 2 1

LIBRARY OF CONGRESS CATALOGING-IN-PUBLICATION DATA
Coman, Carolyn.
Bee and Jacky / Carolyn Coman.
p. cm.
Summary: Thirteen-year-old Bee resumes the physical relationship she has had in the past with her seventeen-year-old brother Jacky, a move that forces them to confront their personal histories.
ISBN 0-14-130637-8 (pbk.)
[1. Incest Fiction. 2. Brothers and sisters Fiction. 3. Emotional problems Fiction. 4. Family problems Fiction.]
I. Title.
PZ7.C729Bg 1999 [Fic]—dc21 99-21469 CIP

Printed in the United States of America

bee

and

jacky

friday

LATE FRIDAY AFTERNOON, Bee's brother Jacky announced that he would not go on the family trip to Decatur. He'd been outside shooting baskets and his T-shirt was yellowed and sweat-stained. Now he was standing at the refrigerator gulping lemonade. "I'm not going tomorrow," he said. "I'm gonna skip it." Bee wheeled to look at him and then at their mother, leaning over the sink shaving carrots. Jacky wiped his mouth with the back of his hand and shoved the refrigerator door closed.

"What do you mean?" Ann Cooney said, carrot and peeler suddenly separate. Bee could hear her sounding frightened, the way she was with Jacky. "Of *course* you're going. We're all going, we planned this. Mom and Dad Cooney are expecting us." They had not visited Bee's grandparents since moving to Fort Wayne, but had lived with them in Decatur for nearly three years after her father was shipped home, hurt, from Vietnam.

"I'm not going," Jacky said again, his voice flat and final. "You can't make me." He shrugged; he was done.

Bee set the knife down next to the spoon, blade facing in as she had been taught. She was still hearing: *You can't make me.*

"Oh, Jacky," her mother said with a nervous giggle, "don't talk like that, honey. It's Labor Day weekend, we've planned this for a long time."

But Jacky was walking away, as he often did after announcing what he would and wouldn't do. He was seventeen and had his driver's license and was a full foot taller than their mother. What he wanted came first.

All *Bee* wanted, as he walked past her, was for him to look at her—just look at her. And he did: a quick glance that didn't tell her much of anything. Still, for just a second it put her with him, on his side, and not part of what he didn't want, wouldn't do. He went into his bedroom and closed the door behind him.

She sighed, studied the place settings, the extra napkin for her father. She felt embarrassed for her mother and how she couldn't win. A moment later she heard the water running, and when she looked up her mother had returned to the carrots, was scraping away.

Bee got out the goblets her mother had collected from the gas station promotion years before and set one at each place, put out the salt and pepper, the butter dish. Once she had finished setting the table, she went to her bedroom and shut *her* door, too.

Bee's room was hot and dry and neat. She was almost fourteen, but her mother still made the bed for her every morning, snapping the bedspread taut across the mattress, no wrinkles or lopsidedness where its fringed edges met the floor. Bee sat on her bed and studied herself, her baby face, in the wicker-framed mirror over the dresser. She had white and delicate skin, easily burned or blotched, like Jacky's, and always looked slightly startled, even to herself. Her puffy upper lip disappointed her, and she thought her chin was weak. Jacky had a chin like hers, but his was covered with hair now—straggles the exact color of Bee's light red curls, just wisps really, not nearly a beard. Bee found it ugly and a little sad.

So what that he wouldn't go with them to Decatur? It wouldn't be the same as when they'd lived there, anyway, when Bee was eight and nine and ten, and her parents were always gone to the VA Hospital for rehab, and she and Jacky were inseparable and endlessly played in the woods behind her grandparents' house.

They played war. They reenacted the ambush that had brought down half the men in their father's platoon, and by themselves tried to change how things had turned out. Bee always played the wounded one, and Jacky the rescuer. Bee lay on her back and imagined all there was of her that could be hit or hurt—enough to keep her body splayed on the ground, tree roots gouging her back, unable even to stand—while she waited for Jacky to save her. Jacky called for more backup on his walkie-talkie, screamed out orders to the medics, marked the spot where the chopper would land to pick up the wounded. Then, after thrashing through the underbrush to get to where Bee had fallen, he dragged her to safety. He told her she would be all right, whatever wounds she had envisioned, however much blood had been lost.

After school, on weekends, all during the sticky summer months, Bee and Jacky escaped to the woods, where even the light was different—darker, fractured—with a climate all its own, denser than the air out in the open. Some days they played their game until the sun went down and they were called in for dinner, where Bee's father struggled even to bring the fork up to his mouth. Her mother said, "Great, Phil. You're doing *fine*," and pulling her chair so close to his that it touched, she mopped up everything he dropped or drooled with a wad of paper towels.

Over time, the wounds Bee imagined in the woods became more grave: damage from shrapnel, bullets, land mines. More and more got blown up, too—her legs, the inside of her head, her whole body. Jacky practically yanked Bee's hair out dragging her to safety, hollered louder, swore, but neither of them abandoned their game until they had to, when they moved.

And now Jacky would not return. Bee remembered: *You can't make me.* She tried to tell herself *So what* again, but she simply could not imagine Decatur without him, could not conjure up the woods without Jacky in them, and the notion of going back alone sat inside her, a brick.

She heard the van that dropped off her father every

night pull into the driveway. He arrived home at 6:10, from his job at Benzi's Chevrolet. The VA had lined it up for him when they moved to Fort Wayne. Bee's mother always had dinner ready to serve, the carrots or beans or broccoli cooked to death.

It was carrots tonight: Bee smelled them as soon as she stepped into the hall. Her father was just coming in the door. He had on a short-sleeved white shirt, his belt cinched tight. "Hi, Dad," she said. When he smiled he looked like he was asking whether he was wearing the right expression. Bee always felt slightly apologetic for making him talk. She thought she pulled him away from someplace inside himself where he was more comfortable being.

They took their places at the table. Bee's mother had delivered the serving dishes, set them down on hotpads, and was asking herself aloud whether she had forgotten anything. Jacky and Bee faced each other, across the middle of the table where it pulled apart to accommodate more leaves. It could seat up to ten but never had.

Phil Cooney cleared his throat and bowed his head. Jacky did not make a move, but Bee watched his face harden. He did not even bother to fold his hands anymore. The rest of the family said grace anyway: Bless us, O Lord, and these Thy gifts which we are about to receive through the bounty of Christ our Lord, Amen. Bee thought that her father's voice sounded like it came from under water.

Her mother sliced the serving spoon into the spaghetti casserole and shook the bottle of salad dressing—creamy Italian with Baco-bits—with her other hand. "Well," she said, as soon as everyone else began to eat, "Jacky has made quite a little decision for himself." She sat straighter in her chair, spoke a bit louder than she needed to. "He has decided—and I think this is *just fine*—that he wants some time to himself before school starts and that he'd like to stay home this weekend. He's worked hard this summer, and I think he's earned a rest."

Jacky was shoveling food as his mother spoke, head down low over his plate, not looking at anybody. It was as if what his mother was saying had nothing at all to do with him. She could have been the TV.

"OK," Bee's father said. He never argued. Except for grace, he rarely said a word at dinner. He just ate. And Bee felt that all she could do for her father was not look: not see how much food stayed on his chin, his shirt, his placemat, not watch his battle with the endless strands of cheese. Why did her mother make so many casseroles? Jacky looked and then turned away, obviously disgusted by what he saw.

"Well, good, then," her mother said, "that's settled," and finally picked up her fork. But before she took her first bite, she suddenly added, "Not that there won't be rules, Jacky. You understand that, I hope. No coming and going at all hours. And you have to eat. Real meals. So don't you think there won't be rules, and . . ." She did not seem to know how to finish.

Jacky was downing milk from his blue goblet. He looked straight past Bee, out the sliding screen door to the cement slab in their backyard where he endlessly practiced basketball, even on the hottest days.

"And no *friends*," her mother said, finally.

For an awful second Bee thought her mother was *describing* Jacky, saying some hurtful, true thing about him right out loud.

"I don't want every teenager in Fort Wayne thinking they can turn our house into one big party . . ."

Then Bee understood that her mother was just making up rules, and she felt a small flood of relief for Jacky, who was still staring off past her. Suddenly his mouth, which was full of noodles, dropped open. It took Bee a moment to realize that he was not responding to anything going on at the dinner table. He was stunned by something he saw outside, and Bee finally twisted around in her seat to find out what it was.

There, not twenty feet away from them, on the cement square where Jacky practiced basketball, stood a bull. It was huge, dense, with a ring in its nose and loops of thick, foamy saliva hanging from the end of its immense head.

Bee dropped her fork.

"My word," Ann Cooney said.

They all—even Bee's father—pushed back their

chairs and went to stand at the sliding screen door to see better. They stood and stared, and for a while the bull barely moved. Then he made heavy, slow shifts of weight. Only his tail moved fast, as if it had a life separate from the rest of him. He lifted a hoof and then set it down, snorted.

"How in God's name ...?" their mother started but did not finish, because the sight of this animal, so close to them and so out of nowhere, had more or less silenced her. Jacky said, "Shit," and got away with it. Finally their father spoke. "Black Angus," he said.

Only Bee remained totally silent, transfixed by the creature she was staring at. Her stillness drew her mother's attention away from the bull.

"Bee?" she said. "Darling?"

Bee could not answer—or move. Jacky and their father looked at her then. Her mother said, again,

quite sharply: "Bee." It was a command, almost.

And no sooner did Bee respond—shudder, breathe, come back—than she fainted, collapsed as if every joint in her body had suddenly folded.

"Oh," Ann cried out as she dropped beside her daughter in nearly the same heartbeat. Bee's father knelt, too. Jacky remained where he was, staring at his kneeling mother and father and at his sister who had fallen down.

Bee did not completely lose consciousness, but inside and out she was toppled, as if that immense, dumb animal had appeared out of nowhere and emptied her of whatever enabled her to stand. The memory of the bull roused her a little and she turned her head to see it again, but in the time it had taken for her to fall down, the bull had trotted away.

Bee's mother put her hands on her daughter's face and pivoted her head away from the window. "Bee, darling," she said. "Are you all right?" She told her husband to get a cool washcloth.

Bee could hear her mother's voice perfectly clearly, see her father rise to do as he'd been told, feel the softness of her mother's hands on her face, but that was all.

"It's all right," her mother said. "It's gone, it can't hurt us."

What her mother said confused Bee. Hurt them? The bull? Would it have?

Her father arrived back with the washcloth and handed it to Bee's mother, who placed it on her forehead. The coolness was a shock, and it returned her skin—her body—to her.

"Can you stand up, honey?" her mother asked. "Let's just get you right into bed." Bee started to obey, leaning forward and beginning to rise, when suddenly—out of nowhere, it seemed—Jacky appeared, filling every bit of space around her. He pressed in toward her, leaning over her, arm extended. And Bee pulled back as if she had touched fire.

Jacky retreated then too, just as quickly, but in the instant they pulled away from each other Bee got a good look at his face: not the disgusted one he wore when the family said grace, or the stunned face that had seen the bull. It was the face she knew from all the times he had come to save her in the woods.

Bee's mother helped her to her bedroom, pulled back the tightly tucked sheet and summer blanket. Bee stepped out of her shorts and flip-flops and climbed into bed, and the cool lightness of the white sheet felt good across her legs. Her mother busied herself with plumping, straightening, picking up Bee's clothes.

After just a few minutes of neatening, her mother announced that she knew what the problem was. "The *heat,*" she said conclusively. "These dog days take a toll after a while." She said she knew just what Bee needed, and left to get ginger ale at the mini-mart.

Bee lay in her bed, relieved to be tucked in, ginger ale on its way. Jacky had gone to his room; her father was somewhere else. She didn't mind being alone. She had the odd feeling that she had *finally* fallen down in front of her entire family, as if she had been meaning to for a long time and had only now gotten around to doing it.

Suddenly her father appeared in the doorway. "You OK, Prize?" he asked. Prize—short for Surprise—was what he had called her when she was a little girl.

Bee nodded, a slight blush rising to her face. She knew her father's ears would turn red if he tried to have an actual conversation; she was shy *for* her father, sometimes.

"OK, then," he said, in his underwater voice, but he did not retreat.

Bee waited.

"I fainted once," he said, speaking to her curtained window.

Bee could hardly believe he was still there, talking.

He gave a little shrug. "Takes it out of you."

Bee lay in her bed and didn't know what to say. Some part of her understood that her father was talking about the war. And she knew that he was trying to tell her something, but she didn't know what, or how to respond. Should she say thank you?

"If you want more water . . ." her father offered, and then he was gone.

Her mother returned with the ginger ale just a few minutes later, fretting about whether Bee would be up to traveling in the morning. Bee surprised them both when she said, "You can't make me." She had taken Jacky's words inside her mouth and now they were spilling out.

"I *beg* your pardon?" her mother snapped, but then retreated just as quickly, because it was obvious that Bee had spoken a foreign language, repeating sounds without necessarily understanding what they meant. "Honey," her mother said, softening. "Don't you *want* to go? Or do you really think you're sick?" She put her hand on Bee's forehead.

Bee didn't know. So she surprised herself once again when she answered, "I can't go, Mom." And it was true: she *couldn't* go back to Decatur without Jacky. She just couldn't.

Every feature on her mother's face contracted.

"Just *what* is going on here?" she said. She pursed her lips, sighed. "Well," she said, turning back to pour the ginger ale, "I suppose we can decide in the morning. But your father and I *have* to go, darling. There's just no way around it." She left Bee alone then, and watched TV with Phil in the family room. Bee heard occasional bursts of canned laughter—mostly her parents watched sitcoms—and those were the sounds she fell asleep to.

Very late that night, Bee awakened to Jacky standing over her. It was his presence, more than any sound, that woke her. And she did not startle as she had when he leaned over her by the sliding screen door. Now, in her dark bedroom, and just as she came out of sleep, his being there felt deeply familiar.

He lay across her, over the sheet. Bee waited for him to say what he was supposed to: *You're hurt.*

Don't move. I'll get you out of this. He said nothing, and his body was heavy on top of hers, much heavier than it had been in the woods.

"I can't move my legs," she whispered. Was that true? It's what she had always said.

Jacky shifted his body so that he was more nearly over her from head to toe. She felt him position himself against her, and shifted her own body, her legs that could not move, to accommodate him.

"I'm hurt bad," she said, eyes closed to remember the treetops, the huge blue sky.

Jacky was not saying his lines. He was not dragging her away, out of range and fire, not pulling her across the risen tree roots, her head bumping on the ground, pine needles and pebbles and dirt clinging to her, staining her clothes. He was moving on top of her, rocking against her, back and then forward, a hard rhythm, breathing hard—as he had in the woods, Bee remembered in that instant. *As he had in the woods.* And then a land mine blew everything to bits, erupted the ground beneath her, fired her bones and brains and memory up to the treetops and the killer blue sky.

After Jacky went back to his room, bits of memory floated down on Bee like ash: her silent, slow-moving grandparents, their big brick house, the pond where she and Jacky fished, where they caught an eel once, and sunfish, some of them with egg-lined bellies. She remembered skating on the pond with Jacky. She remembered a neighborhood dog named Geronimo who crashed through the ice. The dog was chasing a hockey puck, and Bee watched as the thin ice at the far end of the pond cracked beneath his weight. She saw how wildly he resisted going under, how he clawed the air, his whole big body tightened against the inevitable plunge, every inch of him scrabbling and pawing and straining against it. She remembered that moment perfectly, over and over and over for all the hours of the night that were left.

saturday

EARLY SATURDAY MORNING, sounds broke through what Bee was remembering. She heard her parents' closet door being pulled back on its rollers, short bursts of water running as her father shaved in the bathroom. Her mother always liked to get a head start when they traveled, and the sun had just risen. She heard her mother go down the hall and into the kitchen, and then the familiar sounds of drawers and bowls and cabinets. Those house sounds, the here and now of them, were a comfort to Bee. They made it seem safe to sleep, and she closed her eyes and dozed. She startled awake just a little while later, and quickly got up and went into the kitchen, surprising her mother.

"Oh!" Ann Cooney said. "Look at you, here you are, are you feeling better?"

Bee did not answer.

"Sweetie?" her mother said, and came over to Bee, and put her hand under Bee's chin. "Are you? All better?"

Bee nodded, a maybe.

"Oh, darling," her mother said. "You're barely awake, you're half asleep. Let me get you some juice. You go sit down."

Bee went over to her place at the dining room table and sat, a little like the sleepwalker her mother said she was.

Ann came back and handed her a small glass of

orange juice. "Daddy and I talked it over," her mother said. "About your staying." She was practically whispering. Jacky's room was right off the dining room, and if their voices woke him, he would yell at them to shut up. "It's all settled," she continued, leaning in toward Bee like a conspirator. "It's fine, it's probably for the best. This way your father and I can see for ourselves how Mom and Dad Cooney are really doing." Bee knew her mother thought there was something wrong with Gramma Cooney. "You and Jacky will be *fine*," she told Bee. "It will be nice." She patted her daughter's hand. "I'm just going to make you some breakfast, bacon and eggs, and then Daddy and I need to get going."

Bee hooked her feet on the rung of the dining room chair and repeated inside her head what her mother had told her: *Daddy and I talked it over* . . . As if, late at night, in their bedroom, her parents talked and talked and talked, told each other every secret there was to tell. Her father whispered about the war, fainting, falling down. Her mother talked about something other than food. They had private jokes. Imagining this world, these other parents, was irresistible, even though Bee did not believe in them. She knew that most nights her father left their bedroom and slept in the family room. He had bad, noisy dreams that Bee's mother called snoring. Still, there was the sound of *Daddy and I talked it over*, and Bee held on to that.

She froze when Jacky opened his bedroom door and stepped out. She couldn't bear to see if he looked at her, just listened as he walked down the hallway and went into the bathroom. Bee's mother set a half grapefruit mounded with sugar at his place for when he came back, and then went to the stove and cracked eggs into the bacon fat to cook.

"Why are we having eggs?" Jacky said when he sat down. They didn't usually have eggs on Saturday.

"Oh, I just thought it would be nice," their mother answered from the stove. "A nice way to start you off." She told him Bee would be staying home, too. "The last thing Mom and Dad Cooney need is for us to bring a little bug into their house. Even if you are feeling better, Bee. The rest will do you good. Both of you." Bee looked at Jacky then. She wanted him to be glad, or relieved, for the news to soften his face, but nothing showed.

"Eat," their mother told them, and Bee and Jacky ate while their father made repeated silent trips to the car and back, loading up trays of food, a fan, a TV antenna, two folding chairs. Ann Cooney ripped lengths of tin foil to cover the muffins and deviled eggs she was bringing to Decatur. "I made a list of everything that's in the refrigerator," she said. "So you can just look and see what there is. *Plenty* of macaroni." She sponged off the counters and declared herself and Phil ready to go. "Don't get up," she told Bee and Jacky. "Finish your eggs. We'll just be on our way and we'll phone tonight." Finally, as they were almost to the door, she called out, "You're in charge, Jacky. You take care of Bee."

Bee stared at her plate of food, the bright yellow of the yolk she had speared. Jacky was already done. He pushed back his plate, got up, and went into his room. A minute later he'd turned on the music and it was throbbing out his door, into the room where Bee sat. Her bare legs were sticky against the chair. It was going to be a hot day. It already was.

She did the dishes and went to her room to get dressed. First she picked up and handled the new, blank school notebooks and binder that were piled on her dresser, ready for school to start. She ran the ziplock across the filmy pencil holder that clipped inside her looseleaf binder. Jacky had been held back, was going to repeat his junior year. Bee was gaining on him. She put on shorts and a T-shirt and then lay across her bed. She felt as heavy—as weighted down—as she ever had in the woods, on her back, wounded on the forest floor.

She could hear Jacky shooting hoops outside. The steady *thump thump thump* of the basketball was a deeply familiar sound to her, as present and unexceptional as the beating of her heart. It continued pulsing in her even after Jacky had stopped and then taken off somewhere in the car. Finally she got up and went into the family room and sat in front of the TV.

Jacky wasn't gone long, and when he returned he had beer: six gold cans stacked together in their cardboard wrapper that he set on the dining room table. Bee saw them when she came into the kitchen, and she put them away in the refrigerator for him, as if that was what she always did, as if it were the most normal thing in the world. Bee liked how the beer momentarily gave her something to do, how real it was, the little slots for her thumb and index finger to lift it by. A six-pack was something any brother and sister would get when their parents left them by themselves for a weekend.

That afternoon Jacky drank the first one, stood in the kitchen and gulped it down and then burped loud enough for Bee to hear in the living room. At dinner—Bee heated up the macaroni and cheese casserole—he drank another two and told Bee to go ahead and have one herself, which she did. It tasted sour to her. She made herself keep drinking, but she really didn't like the taste. The beers seemed to loosen Jacky, though—gave him an easy laugh and more words than he usually had for her.

She asked him what he thought school would be like. He said he didn't give a shit about school, that he was through with school anyway. Bee wasn't listening too carefully to what he was saying because she was thinking about what she could say next to keep the conversation going. She felt like she was practicing, playing grown-up, but it was more than just a game because their parents really were gone and it was real beer they were drinking. "Do you drink beer a lot?" she asked respectfully.

"Nah," he said.

She didn't think he did.

"Whenever I want," he said.

"Daddy never does," she said. She couldn't believe she said *Daddy*. She sounded like such a baby to herself.

"He never does *shit*," Jacky said.

Bee tightened a little inside. She didn't want their time together, talking, to be over, but she didn't know where to go from there, from *He never does shit.* She couldn't think of any way to continue, or to say it wasn't so.

"He's a jerk," Jacky said. "A fuckin' loser."

Bee held still. This was the most Jacky had talked to her in a long time. What he was saying didn't matter.

"Can't even get it up anymore," Jacky said.

Bee just looked at him.

"Whydaya think he sleeps out there?" he said, disgusted, and he motioned toward the family room by jutting out his chin.

Bee was holding on to Jacky's voice and how he was talking to her, including her. *Don't stop, please.*

When he popped open the third can she was relieved. She said to him, “Why wouldn’t you go to Gramma and Grampa’s, really?”

He made a spitting sound, made an exaggerated face. “Gimme a fuckin’ break,” he said. “Why the hell should I go there? That fuckin’ place.” Bee memorized how he spat out the first syllable of *fuckin’*.

All of a sudden he wasn’t talking anymore. Had he answered her? Was it her turn? She didn’t know, and before she could think of what to say or do, he stood up and walked outside.

The sliding screen door smacked shut behind him and Bee felt it like a slap. She wanted to cry. Instead she stood up and started clearing the table, as if it were a regular dinner and when people went away it was time to clean up.

She rinsed the dishes and loaded them into the dishwasher. But her whole body ached, as it had all those months and months when they were playing their game, all the times Jacky had come to save her, to cover her body with his and tell her, "You're hurt. Don't move. I'll get you out of this." When he flattened her against the ground and the tree roots with all his pushing, rammed his body against hers. When no matter how tight she held on, he went away from her—she could feel him leaving her—even as he gripped her bony shoulders and called out, "Oh, God!" She had tried, then, to follow him where he went, but she ended up lost herself: in a place with no one and nothing except for the tops of the trees.

Jacky was shooting baskets and the *thump thump thump* of the bouncing pounded inside Bee now, as if the volume of her own heartbeat had been turned up. She followed the sound outside and sank into a plastic chaise lounge to the left of the cement slab. She needed help to support her body.

Lying down, she watched her brother in the left-over heat of the day, with the plastic strips of the chaise lounge pinching at the backs of her legs and the sunlight so fractured it was impossible to see straight. In all the times she had seen Jacky practicing through the window, heard him, *known* that that was what he was doing, she had never actually gone outside just to watch him.

Jacky had on long, loose shorts that caught on his hips, below the waist. He was sweating freely, hopping, jumping, laying up, catching the rebound. For ten minutes or more he kept on shooting and paid no attention to Bee at all. Suddenly, though, he spun to face her and said, "What're *you* looking at?"

Bee had no words. Finally, with effort, she said, "You."

Jacky dribbled the ball a few times. "Yeah," he said. "Well, *don't*," and then he turned, jumped, sent the ball flying. It hit the rim of the hoop and bounced back.

His words ricocheted inside Bee's head, and the sunlight pressed down on her, on the ugly green and white plastic woven strips of the chair. She could go inside, she knew; she could get some iced tea. That was on her mother's list, taped to the refrigerator door: *iced tea, green pitcher.*

Instead she studied the furrow that ran down the back of Jacky's neck, watched his working shoulder blades. Her aching body remembered his. Her chest remembered his chest, her legs his legs, between her legs between his legs, where they fit together, how the rubbing felt.

Jacky kept dribbling, one, two, three, taking shots, missing a lot. "Beat it," he called to her, not even bothering to turn his head.

Bee didn't move. She let his words dissolve, never

taking her eyes off him. She sat in the sucking heat, watched Jacky and how he moved, watched so intensely that for an instant her vision disconnected his body from itself and everything else in the world, into just arms and legs and fingers and calves, jumping and pushing and suspended in the Indiana air and heat, no past, no future, no story, as if Jacky himself did not even exist.

He threw a wild shot, and it bounced wide off the backboard, onto the grass, near her feet. Bee heard the rustle-crackle of the grass as the ball rolled across it, on its way to her. She instinctively bent down to retrieve it and when she sat up and faced Jacky, the ball in her hands, she saw the bear.

It had come out of nowhere, huge, brown, matted, angry as sin, bigger than Jacky by three heads, and wide enough to encircle him entirely. Instantly and from behind, the bear wrapped itself around

Jacky in a horrible embrace, its claws crisscrossing before they raked open his chest, cracking apart his rib cage and exposing, underneath, as if it had been hiding, his heart.

There was blood all over. She would have screamed, but there was only one sound in the whole world, an ocean of sound, and that was the bear's roar.

She managed to stand, get out of the chaise lounge, and move herself away. She did not look back at Jacky but crossed the sun-baked yard and pulled open the sliding screen door and stepped inside the darker, cooler house. She stood still for just a second, waiting to see if she would vomit or not.

The phone rang. The sound jolted her, had never been quite so loud. It rang a second time, and she went over and answered it.

"Bee? We're he-ere," her mother said, sing-song.

"I'm just calling to let you know we're here."

Bee nodded.

"Are you there, honey?"

"Yes," Bee said, still nodding.

"And everything's OK? How's Jacky, what's he doing?"

Bee almost turned to look outside, but she didn't. "He's shooting baskets," she told her mother.

"*Naturally*," her mother laughed. "What else? Well, you tell him to take it easy. It's awfully hot, it's really *too* hot." Then she told Bee that Mom and Dad Cooney sent their love and said they hoped she felt better. She said she would call again tomorrow.

"OK," Bee said, and hung up the phone. She went down the hallway and into her bedroom and sat on her bed and stared at her curtains. Then she laid her body down and closed her eyes and went to a place that was deeper than sleep.

saturday night

BEE AWOKE HOURS LATER, parched, her open mouth sucking in air. She didn't even know where she was. She woke up wanting, but she didn't know what, exactly. Everything she awakened to—thirst, wanting, deep confusion—had already taken hold of her as she slept, so opening her eyes didn't change anything. Where was everyone?

Her clock said 1:47. She had slept in her shorts and sleeveless shirt, lying on top of her bed. Now she was chilled and felt dirty. She got up and put on her nightgown in the dark, and deeply, angrily wished that she hadn't fallen asleep early and woken up at so the wrong time, past midnight and still far from morning. She felt outside the night and didn't want to be.

She stepped into the dark hallway. Her parents were gone, she remembered. To Decatur. The bathroom light was still on, and the one in the kitchen, and the mix of lights that were on and lights that were off felt creepy to her, made everything seem unfinished. Why hadn't Jacky turned them off when he went to bed? Where was he? She hurried down the hallway suddenly, as if there were something coming up behind her, and she went into the bathroom and closed the door.

She saw her scared face in the mirror and looked down, then drank two glasses of cold water from the red plastic cup that matched the soap dish and the toothbrush holder. Now she was sorry she had closed the door, because she knew she would have to open it and go back out. Part of her wanted just to keep going in the other direction: step into the bathtub and crawl out the window above it, into the yard and through the bushes into their neighbor's yard and then through their yard and on and on, straight ahead, never turning around. But how could she do that? She *couldn't*; she had to turn off the lights and go back to her bedroom and try to get to sleep again. She opened the bathroom door and stood absolutely still, listening for whatever sounds someone or something hiding might make.

She heard nothing.

In slow motion she took one step out of the bath-room. To her left she could see into her parents' dark bedroom, the outline of their twin beds, neatly made, and everything in order. For a moment she concentrated on her mother's nightstand table and what she knew was inside its drawer: emery boards, manicure scissors, a little blue prayer book, cough drops. She tried hard to think only about those things—those real, little objects that she could picture, that she had handled and smelled—but she couldn't hold on to them now because something else was pushing its way into her mind, forcing everything else out.

She rushed down the hall, straight past her bedroom and into the dining room. The kitchen was all lit up. Jacky had made popcorn, and the pan and bowl and a beer can were all out on the counter and there was an oily smell to everything.

She looked at the dishes and she did not look at Jacky's closed door, to her right. Her heart was racing. The memory was coming, lumbering down the hallway toward her, and she stepped deeper into the room, and then deeper, until she was at Jacky's door. She had to keep going, so she turned the knob and slipped inside. His room was dark and silent. She went and stood by his bed, saw the mound his sleeping body made on the mattress. She didn't make a sound or move, or even breathe, but her heart was hammering, and then he shifted his body, leaned up on his elbow, and said to her, "What do you want?"

What did she *want*? Was *that* the question? She didn't know. But words came out of her mouth. "It's all right," she told him. More words came to her, inside her head: *You're hurt. Don't move. I'll get you out of this*. Yes, of course: it was Jacky's turn to be saved, and she had come to save him. It could be bad, she told herself: there could be claw marks all over him. His chest could be split down the middle, his heart exposed.

Jacky lay back and Bee draped her body across him and covered him. She felt his chest with her hand, the place where he had been ripped open. But there were no marks there, just his skin, and none across his shoulders either, or his neck, just smooth, taut skin and strands of muscle beneath it. She felt along his side, along the ripple of his rib cage, into the invitation of his hip. She slid her hand across the dry cotton of his underwear. She was feeling for everything: claw marks, openings, hardness she could position herself against. She matched her body over his, covered him with the space she had for him, and began her own moving: on him, as he had moved on and against her so many times, all those times in the woods. *You're hurt. Don't move. I'll get you out of this.* Jacky's words, and now hers.

But Jacky was not holding still, as she always had for him. He had reached down and yanked his underpants lower, taken away what little they had between them, was pulling at her nightgown full of blue flowers and twisting it around her. He could move everything, nothing was broken—his arms were around her and his legs were entwining hers. He was moving Bee, trying to position her, forcing her beneath him. And as he did, she felt tree roots rising up into her back and hurting her, she felt them digging in between her shoulder blades, knotted and unforgiving, and she could not stand it.

You can't make me, everything inside her called out. She would not go back there again, to the forest floor, endlessly waiting and then left behind, hurt, millions of fallen pine needles living on her, marking her. She pushed up and against Jacky with all her might, pounding on his chest with her fists until he grabbed her wrists, and they fought, wild and frantic, close to plunging themselves right off Jacky's bed.

Bee felt it coming: deep inside their thrashing against each other she felt the awful, inevitable fall coming. And just when it seemed absolutely imminent, unstoppable, she lunged forward and swung her arm over Jacky and turned on the lamp on his bedside table.

The light was sudden and terrible. It hurt her.

They drew back toward the center of the bed but away from each other, squinting against the brightness.

Bee held still, blinking, and as her eyes adjusted, she saw only a portion of Jacky's chest, the landscape of a few ribs. She gradually looked up to his face. He was rubbing his eyes with his thumb and index finger, hard, unkindly. They lay like that, just breathing fast, for a few moments. Then Bee drew up one leg, slowly, and carefully climbed over him, dismounting, as if she were scaling a fence, lifting her leg higher than she needed to so that she would not touch or graze him, until she finally stood beside his bed, where she had started out. Her nightgown hung straight on her again, above her knees, wrinkled.

They were not in the woods, she saw. She was standing in Jacky's room—had come there herself—and his things were all around her, piles of magazines, huge sneakers, his bed that he had had since he was a boy, the one with remnants of stickers still on the headboard.

Jacky continued to rub his eyes. Then he rolled over, into the wall, his back to her, as far away as he could go.

Bee stared at him and saw that there were no marks on his body, no cuts or even scars. Just her brother Jacky's back. His underpants were pulled down and his bottom was exposed, the flat halves there for her to see, as if he'd had a spanking. Now Jacky's soft, freckled back was moving and she watched it shaking, quivering, up into his shoulders, until finally she understood that he was crying.

She did not know what to do, and her not knowing felt like a well she could fall down into forever. *Touch him*, something inside her said—his back, the part that was crying. But she couldn't, as if she were broken and could not lift her hand, not even to comfort.

Then everything seemed lost, and she turned and walked into the dining room, the linoleum cool and sticky against her bare feet. The popcorn stuff still sat. The sliding screen door was open to her right, and the lights were on, but she saw no reason to lock up or turn off lights now.

She left Jacky's door open behind her and walked to her bedroom and lay down on her bed. She did not bother to close her eyes; she was not going to sleep, or to remember the treetops and how they looked against the Decatur sky. The endless loop of Geronimo crashing through the ice would not carry her through the night, either. What she had inside her now, and instead, was what she had seen in Jacky's room—herself, standing by his bed; herself and that she had gone there; his back, exposed; her hand, unable to comfort.

She remembered the sound she had made clicking on the light next to Jacky's bed. It reminded her of the cracking noise trees made in the terrible cold, as if they were snapping apart inside their own trunks. She used to hear that sudden, hollow sound in the woods as she lay on her back, waiting for Jacky to come and save her.

sunday

EARLY THE NEXT MORNING Bee listened as Jacky went down the hall to the bathroom. He was going to leave, she knew—take off somewhere—and just a few moments later she heard the front door open and close and then the car squealing out of the driveway. She lay still in her bed for a long time after he'd gone, waiting—for anything.

Finally she got up and went into the living room and looked at the empty driveway and street. She did not feel inside the day any more than she had felt inside the night, and suddenly *she* wanted to take off, too, the way Jacky had, to be gone. But she couldn't; she was there, in the house, alone, and the aloneness gave a slightly vibrating quality to everything.

She began pacing, moving around the room, touching things, picking them up and putting them down again—framed photographs, magazines on the table, the glass figurines—the way she had fingered her school supplies in her bedroom the day before. She was touching everything, running her hand along each object, registering every bump and texture.

Finally she raised her hands up and touched herself. She felt above her small breasts, near her collar bone. There, through the soft cotton of her nightgown, in a place she had never thought to look, she found the wounds, the gouging.

Her hands flew away from what they had discovered, and she froze, horrified. But then, slowly and deliberately, she made herself touch her body again, pressed the cloth down against her flesh. She couldn't tell for sure how bad it was. She turned her back to the picture window in the living room and slid her shaking hand under her nightgown, between her breasts, and felt the tearing across her chest. She stopped breathing while she felt what was there: many marks, all over her. Finally there was nothing left to do but look at them, and she pulled up her nightgown and revealed the crisscross ruts on her belly. *All right*, she told herself. *This has happened.* She took a breath and lifted her nightgown over her head and let it drop to the floor. Then she looked down on her torso, torn and ripped apart.

She looked at herself for a long time, and next Bee put her finger, her index finger, into one of the ruts, a trough, and felt the blood and the mushy flesh. Then she reached around to her side, over her rib cage, as far around to her back as she could stretch her arm. She did not feel cuts there—she felt protrusions, ropes and knots beneath her skin, molding it from underneath. She crept her fingers up and down her back, feeling for the map of whatever ran across it. With her arms wrapped across her chest, feeling her back, she walked down the hallway, leaving her nightgown behind on the carpet, and went into her parents' room, to stand in front of the large mirror that attached to the back of her mother's dresser. The rake marks she saw across the front of her body came as no surprise: the very wounds she had seen on Jacky, and that even in so short a time she had come to accept in herself. What she needed to see now was her back—and she turned and twisted her head around so that she could take in as much as possible. She saw a network of roots traveling across and up and down it, balls and knots pushing up, hard and gnarled. She climbed onto her mother's bed to see how the roots traveled down through her buttocks into the backs of her legs, down into her ankles, clusters of pine needles sticking to everything—her elbows, the backs of her knees, in her hair.

She turned to face the mirror and her raked-open chest. Once again she began feeling her body, certain spots, each wound with its own contour, crouching on her mother's bed so that she could touch her ankles and calves, then straightening as she molded her hands along her thighs, belly, chest, ran her fingers into her hair, squeezed it at the roots until pine needles rained out and delicately fell around her feet, onto the bedspread.

And finally Bee began to cry. "Look!" she called out. *Look at me.* Not that her body had been so beautiful, so perfect—she knew that she was skinny, that her breasts were hardly more than buds, that she was freckled—but it had been *hers*, hadn't it? Her *body*. And look what had happened to it. Look.

She climbed off the bed and stumbled out into the hallway. She could barely walk for the weight of misery that had come over her. She began to moan, crying loudly, her knees almost buckling. How would she ever make it back? Even to the end of the hallway? She didn't know. "Oh, God," she cried out. "Oh, God."

She put her hand against the wall to steady herself and stay upright, and kept going. Crying out the whole way, she made it to the end of the hall, living room to her left, her nightgown lying in a strip of sunlight that shot across the carpet, and dining room to her right, with its sliding screen door and the backyard beyond.

She walked around the dining room table and pulled open the door, stepped out naked into the hot, dry air, the stunning sunlight. She did not feel the burned grass stabbing at the soles of her feet as she crossed to the cement slab where Jacky endlessly shot baskets, where the bull had appeared, where she had seen the bear. Stepping onto its pebbled hotness, she stood and hung her head, weeping, as she descended to a place inside herself that felt terribly bad, where it felt like *she* was badness itself. "Oh," she cried out, over and over. "Oh." She wept for a long time, falling as far as there was for her to fall.

And then she began to burn. Small blue flames erupted on the tops of her feet, from between her toes, on her chest, inside her belly. She watched them grow with every breath she took, shooting up and uniting with one another, spreading, engulfing her inside and out, into one huge, exquisite flame. Part of it, and within its roar, Bee surrendered to the immensity of her sorrow and shame, to everything she saw and didn't see, to the fire.

And when the burning was done, Bee was left standing, as she had been, on the cement slab, naked. Her crying slowed and then stopped. Little by little she experienced a lightness in herself, an absence of weight, traveling out to her muscles and bones, fingers and toes, to the very top of her head. The emptying sensation rocked her, as if she'd been playing tug-of-war and the other side had finally let go and sent her reeling. But she didn't fall down. She drew herself up and took a filling breath. She felt space between all her ribs, along the whole length of her spine; she felt delivered from what she could not carry alone.

"Thank you," she said out loud, even though

there was no one there and she was still deep inside herself. But she could breathe. And she did nothing but stand and breathe, in and out, until after a while, without thinking, she crossed her arms and hooked her hands over her shoulders, let her head drop to the side. Then she began patting herself lightly on her shoulders, the way, when she babysat, she patted the children who cried and wanted their mothers. Now she felt the warmth of her own hands on her own shoulders, and took comfort.

She was standing like that—holding herself—when Jacky stepped into the yard, saw her, and screamed. "Bee! Bee! Jesus *Christ*, Bee," he hollered. "What're you doing? What the fuck are you *doing*?" He was charging toward her, and Bee watched him, recognized him, felt that he was galloping over to her from a great distance. She was not afraid. "Oh, *shit*,

Bee," he said. He stopped just short of her and extended both arms straight out—to her? She couldn't tell. It looked like he was telling her to stop, but she was standing completely still. "Bee," he said, more quietly but in great agitation, "what're you doing?" He shifted from foot to foot, the way the bull had.

"Bee," Jacky was saying, "you gotta come inside. You can't do this. You can't be out here." Bee looked at him. He flicked his wrist and motioned back toward the house. "Come on, Bee. Get inside."

When she didn't move at all he began hopping and shaking his hands. "Oh *fuck*, oh fuck": Bee heard the words he was saying. What mattered to her, though, was how his face was twisting up, the way his eyes were, his crumpled forehead. She saw what it was: fear. Jacky was really badly afraid.

"BEE." He was screaming at her now.

She knew that face. Was it hers? No, it was his,

his face when he got scared. "What's the *matter,* Jacky?" she blurted out.

He froze and looked at her, amazed, as if he didn't know she could speak. After a moment, he said, wide-eyed and very quietly and cautiously, "You have to come inside, Bee."

"OK," she said. She did not want him to be afraid. But she did not make a move.

"OK?" Jacky repeated, and then he reached out, pulled Bee's arm away from her chest, and took her hand in his. He led her off the court and across the yard. She could feel her hand in his, and she liked it.

As soon as they stepped into the house he turned to her and said, "You have to get dressed." Now that they were inside, he didn't look as scared as he had, as absolutely terrified. "Can you get dressed?" he said. "Want me to get you some clothes?"

"Yes," she answered. She could tell that he wanted the answer to be yes.

"OK," he said, and took off to her room and came back just a minute later with a T-shirt and shorts bunched up in his hand. "Here," he said, poking them out to her in his fist.

She took them from him and held them.

"Go on," he said. "Put them on."

She looked down at the shorts and shirt.

"Get *dressed*, Bee," Jacky said to her.

It finally registered on Bee that she was holding clothes—that word, *clothes*, came to her. But what she saw, looking straight down, past the bundle of navy blue and white cotton she held in her hands, were her toes, her bare, skinny, white feet. She dropped the clothes in disbelief and bent forward to see more: her ankles, with just their normal bumps of bone, no knots or bulges, no pine needles, no roots. She saw that her calves were smooth, too, and her knees and thighs. Her hand rose instinctively to her chest—surely that would still have the marks, the cuts. She felt, instead, her breast bone. She looked down and saw her breasts, her nipples, her freckled chest. She was naked, she could see that, but being naked was not what amazed her. She was not torn apart! She was not scorched! She saw her body, whole and fresh, her arms and legs and torso, and it was stunning to her, and harder to believe than her body covered with wounds.

"Bee," Jacky said. She heard him calling to her.

She looked up at him, and though she could not speak, her face, her entire being, spoke, *Oh my God!*

Jacky had picked up the clothes off the floor, was once again holding them out to her. His face was pleading: *Keep going*, it said, *get dressed*, and Bee did not understand. Why should her body be covered *now*?

"Come on," he said to her, urgent and desperate, and then, suddenly, Bee *did* understand: Jacky was not seeing what she saw. He did not see that she was uncut, not bleeding, that she was solid and smooth, that her body was beautiful, how full of light she was. He only saw that she had taken off her clothes. And he wanted her to put them back on, the clothes he was holding out to her. He waggled them in front of her again. "Oh!" she said, coming to attention, surprised by his nearness and by the things around her—the dining room table, the chairs—surprised to be back inside the day.

She reached out and took the shorts from Jacky and stepped into them, and then took the shirt, put it over her head, and threaded her arms through the sleeves. *There*, she thought, once she was dressed. *Is this better?*

But Jacky was not looking at her. Now that Bee was dressed, he stared only at the floor. His face was red, the vein on his neck was pulsing. What did he want now, she wondered. Suddenly it struck Bee as funny—how much trouble they had just trying to be together—and she laughed. Jacky looked up, frightened, so she stopped.

After a long time of standing silent, she shyly asked him, "Where'd *you* go?"

Jacky shrugged. "Nowhere," he said, and then, "Out. I got something to eat."

"Oh." *Out*, she repeated to herself. She began to circle the dining room table, not on her way anywhere, just moving.

Jacky spoke to her back. "You OK, Bee?" he asked.

"Mm-hmm," she answered, nodding her head. Was

she? She didn't know. But she liked how he had spoken to her—*You OK, Bee?*—how normal it sounded, and how he had used her name.

"Do you want something?" he asked. "To drink?"

Bee remembered the ginger ale her mother had bought for her, the water her father had offered to get, a hundred years ago, after she fell down. But she hadn't fallen down this time, she realized. "I'm fine," she told Jacky.

His face broke then. "What *happened*?" he cried out, a child, too loud, begging, asking everything.

He sounded so lost to Bee—he might as well have called out, *Where am I?*—and his voice pierced her. "Oh, Jacky," she said.

But Jacky was already hurrying back from how he had wailed. Bee watched his broken face reassemble. "So what do you want to do?" he said to her after a while, quietly, his voice deeper.

How to answer him. “Have lunch?” Bee tried.

“Are *you* hungry?” he said.

“No.”

They were silent a while more and then Jacky said, "I’m supposed to mow the lawn.” He was biting the inside of his cheek. “You wanna come?” he asked, as if the backyard were some faraway place.

"OK,” she said, and they went out. She stayed put against the sliding screen door and he walked over to the lawn mower and started it up, a great, instant racket. The noise was oddly comforting to Bee, accompaniment to all she was doing: leaning against the door, watching Jacky crisscross the lawn. He made neat rows of mown grass against the unmown, a changing and visible measure of what had been done and what remained to be done. She felt as if *she* had done something—or maybe that something had been done to her—and little by little she let herself rest in between everything that had already happened and everything else that would.

After a while, she took the green hose that was looped around a metal holder next to the sliding door and started spraying the tall, boxy bushes that enclosed their yard. She liked having something to hold and to do, spraying onto and in between the bushes, watching the dry earth soak up all it could, and when it was full, the puddles that formed.

She watered for a long time as Jacky mowed the lawn behind her. She used her thumb to make higher and higher arches of spray, holding the hose with her smooth, unblemished hand, the water turning to diamonds in the sunlight until Jacky made his final pass and shut the mower off.

She heard him walking up behind her, turned, and in turning saw only his feet: he was barefoot. She could hear their mother: *Shoes, Jacky. Shoes.*

What do you think those blades would do to your toes? His feet were stained green and had little clumps of mown grass all over them. They looked funny to her, not like feet at all, and Bee turned the hose and sprayed water across them, whooshing away the grass, splashing back and forth across them until they were washed clean. Then she looked up and there was Jacky, right in front of her, and she might as well have been four or five or six, ready to raise the hose and let her older brother have it—soak him, drench him, show no mercy. She laughed, and so did he. "Forget it," he said. She raised her eyebrows and tilted her head like she was undecided, made one more pass over his feet, and then tossed the hose down on the grass and turned the water off at the faucet.

Jacky asked her if she was hungry, if she wanted to eat. She said sure. They went inside and Jacky ordered a large hamburg and mushroom pizza from Demetroff's—her favorite, not his. First he said he'd pick it up, but just before he hung up he changed his mind and told them to deliver. Bee could tell he didn't know if it was OK to leave her alone or even bring her out in public, because she had taken off her clothes. She remembered that and looked down at her T-shirt and shorts, there where they belonged, on her body that was not burned or torn apart. The pizza arrived about twenty minutes later, and they put the warm, white cardboard box on the kitchen counter and ate there.

"You want something to drink?" Jacky asked. He was serving her.

"Milk," she said, and he got her a glass. He asked her again, right as they were finishing up the pizza, "So you're OK, right?"

Bee looked at him, her soft-faced brother with his

straggly goatee, and she shrugged, a little embarrassed. She didn't know what OK was, what it meant, exactly. "I hope," she finally said. It was the best she could offer, and it was true.

Jacky cleared.

A sweet tiredness filled Bee for the rest of the afternoon. She curled up in her father's chair in the family room, and the sense of simply being done for the moment covered her like a blanket. Jacky stayed close by. He brought her iced tea when he got some for himself, asked what TV show she wanted to watch, didn't leave. Bee knew it wouldn't last forever—the peace—but she felt a secret safe inside her, behind the sheerest veil, resting somewhere in her memory. And there was nothing she had to do—think about it, say what it was, figure it out. Holding it inside her was enough. Every now and then she crisscrossed her arms and patted her smooth, warm skin with her hands, more and more willing to believe what was there and what wasn't.

She and Jacky watched more TV together that night, Bee once again snuggled into her father's chair. They didn't talk much, and that was all right.

When the phone rang during *Bonanza*, Bee was curled up, eyes closed, half-drifting. Jacky answered on the first ring. She listened to Jacky's end of the conversation—"Hi. Yeah. Nothing"—and knew for sure that he was talking to their mother, because his words were flat and dry as a piece of paper. "No, no, she's asleep. OK, yeah." She opened her eyes to look at him, just to see that there was more than what she was hearing.

Jacky was looking at *her,* and Bee was surprised by how much his face and his eyes held—such sadness—when his voice was so flat. "OK," he said to their mother, and then, with just a hint of inflection, "Bye." He hung up the phone. He covered over what Bee had seen in his face, and did not say a word.

"Who was that?" Bee said, just to make him speak.

"Guess," he answered. Sour.

"How are Gramma and Grampa?"

"How should I know?"

He always had to get mad. One little phone call. "Well, what did she say?"

"Nothing."

"*Nothing*?"

There was a car commercial on. "She always says nothing," Jacky said.

Bee heard her mother's voice inside her head, the prattle of it, the nervousness. "She's scared, Jacky," Bee said.

Jacky looked at her.

"Of you."

Jacky shook his head. "Forget it," he said. *Bonanza* was coming back on.

"The *same* as you," Bee said, at the very moment she realized it. She remembered Jacky's face when he found her naked, and later, his voice crying out, *What happened?*

His face right now was a warning. "The same as me *what*?"

"Afraid," Bee said. "You're both afraid."

Jacky lunged forward in his chair. "What're you *talking* about?" he practically yelled at her. "God," he said, more quietly, "don't get *crazy* again."

Bee looked at him. He didn't see what she saw. "I won't," she said. "I'm *not*."

labor day

BEE SLEPT WELL AND LATE, then got up and went into the kitchen. Jacky had cleaned off the table and counter and emptied the trash. She took an orange from the fruit bowl and sat at the table and peeled it. The skin made a little tugging sound as she pulled it back from the fruit, and drops of juice squirted out onto her fingers. Jacky was already outside, practicing. There was a breeze coming through the screen door, and it felt good.

Her parents arrived home before noon, and Bee

went out to greet them in the driveway. Jacky came too. Their mother had driven, as usual, and she called out brightly, "Hel-lo." Their father gave one of his goofy waves, keeping his hand low, down by his leg. They were exactly who they were: that was the funny impression Bee had when she saw them, and she was glad they were home. It seemed like they had been gone forever. Now they were back and the world had changed even though everything in it looked the same, and she had no words for the things she had seen. She helped carry in some of the stuff they had brought back, and her flip-flops made a pleasant clapping sound on the walkway as she made trips back and forth, like a slow and rhythmic little round of applause in the distance.

Her father put away all the things that went in the garage. Even from another room in the house Bee could feel him standing there, in his place, stacking things neatly in the corner, or sitting on the old couch they had stored there years ago.

Her mother put food away and never left the kitchen. She started immediately to get things ready for later, commenting on what Bee and Jacky had and hadn't eaten, talking about Mom and Dad Cooney, just going on, keeping herself company with her own voice. She'd brought back short ribs from Decatur, for them to barbecue. And she was going to make three-bean salad. "Which Jacky won't *touch*," she announced.

Bee stayed with her mother in the kitchen and listened to her talk for a while. Then she went out in the living room and started work on a jigsaw puzzle that Gramma and Grampa Cooney had sent back for her—a New England sawmill scene, 1000 pieces. She sat on the floor at the coffee table, with her legs stretched out underneath it, and found all the straight-edged pieces to make the border. After a while Jacky came out and asked her what she was doing.

"Guess," she said, but she was glad that he had come out of his room and was talking to her. "Wanna help?" she asked.

"Puzzles are pathetic," he said.

She shrugged and locked two corner pieces together.

"People who *do* puzzles are pathetic," he said, and they both laughed. Jacky sat down behind her on the couch. After a little while, when he hadn't said anything else or picked up a magazine and she could feel him just sitting there, she turned and said, "What?"

He looked at her for a second. "Nothing," he said, but clearly it wasn't nothing, he wasn't saying *something*. She concentrated on the puzzle spread out before her and felt him behind her, how filled up he was with whatever he wasn't saying. Maybe he would talk to her back, she thought. She became intensely aware of her back, the light layer of her T-shirt across it, pictured its curve as she leaned over the table, remembered Jacky, rolled away from her, against the wall, his back shaking as he cried. But Jacky didn't say another word, and a while later Bee's mother called out from the kitchen that she should come and set the table, that the coals were ready and her father was putting on the ribs.

They sat down to dinner around five, and almost as soon as they began eating, Jacky announced, "I'm joining the Marines," one little rib pinched between his hands, his head low over his plate. "I decided."

The silence that followed his announcement was enormous—Bee thought it was big enough for the bull to walk into, or the bear, but nothing happened. It was just them, her family, around the table.

"Jacky," her mother said. Her scared, giggly voice. "What do you mean, darling?"

"I'm enlisting," he said, not looking at her.

Bee thought: this is what you didn't tell me but wanted to. That was more important to her, right then, than *what* Jacky was saying. But a beat later, it hit—his news, what he was going to do—and then she was just confused. Was there another Vietnam for him to go to, some place where everything got blown up? She didn't know where or if there were wars going on. She'd been quizzed on that in social studies, in current events, but it hadn't mattered then.

"What about school?" her mother said.

"I'm done with school," Jacky answered. His words were dead.

Bee's mother was patting the base of her blue

goblet, she was practically vibrating. "Oh, Jac-ky," she finally blurted out, several syllables to his name, because she was starting to cry.

Bee watched Jacky's face clench against his mother even as he warned her, in flat, dead words, "Don't cry."

Ann Cooney covered her face with her hands, her shoulders pumping.

"Shut *up*," Jacky ordered, although his mother's crying was nearly silent.

Then, from under water, from the other end of the table, a million miles away, Bee's father said, "Don't speak to your mother like that."

Everyone stared at him, stunned. Bee felt a sucking pull to her father's end of the table, as if the floor had dropped down several inches to the place where he sat. She was surprised that the salt and pepper, the platter of ribs, weren't sliding toward him, heading straight into his lap. His face was taut, as if he were pressing up against an invisible plate of glass, and there was a dribble of barbecue sauce on his chin that looked like blood.

"*What?*" Jacky whispered. Bee felt the force of his attention locking on to their father, as he leaned in and said again, louder and disbelieving, "*What?*"

Bee stopped breathing. Jacky looked close to launching out of his chair. And then what? Would he hit something? Someone? Would he hit their father? Bee thought he might, she saw that he had it in him.

"You're telling me what to *do*? *You're* telling *me*?"

Jacky *was* hitting their father, Bee thought—pounding him on his face and shoulders, nailing him into his chair. "Who the fuck are *you*?" Jacky yelled, his fists on the table. "What the hell do you know about *anything*?" He was inflating before

Bee's eyes, becoming rounder and bigger, pumped up by his rage, like an inner tube getting filled up and fat. "You can't talk to me, you can't say one word to me. So you just shut up, you hear me? You just . . . *shut . . . up.*"

Bee thought he might explode, that his eyes might pop out of his head. She willed her father to sit absolutely still, because she knew that if he moved, if he even raised his head and looked at Jacky, her brother would hit him. He would have to hit him.

"Don't you talk to me," Jacky called out finally, each word ragged. "You stay the fuck away." His voice cracked on what he said last, and he turned from his father. Bee saw Jacky full face then, his terrible face.

"Jacky," Bee's mother begged. "Please."

But Jacky was already stopping himself—his

voice breaking had stopped him—and now he was starting to deflate, trying to get his racing breath and his shaking body under control.

Bee realized that she was shaking, too, that her legs were jackhammering away under the table. Everything around her had gone inside her and was shaking her like a rattle. She reminded herself to breathe, and she breathed. She put her feet flat on the floor and pressed her hands on the tops of her thighs to stop the shaking.

Everyone sat in silence. Then Bee's mother cautiously began, "We know you don't mean that, Jacky. Of course you don't mean that, you would never speak that way to your father." It sounded like some sort of memorized prayer or poem she was starting up. "You don't mean that," she said again. "Everybody's had a long weekend, and the *heat* . . ." Bee watched her mother reciting, her words like water she could wash her hands in. "Getting back to school is always hard . . ."

Bee and Jacky looked at each other across the table while their mother went on talking.

"I gotta go," he said, only to Bee. "I have to get out of here," he pleaded, close to crying, and like he was begging her to see.

She did see: her brother sitting across from her, grinding his teeth to keep his chin from trembling. She saw him clawing his way up and out of frigid water, striking out at everything, wild. She saw that they were *all* hurt—not just her, not just in wars, whether it showed on their bodies or not. She remembered Jacky's back, crying, she remembered him in her bedroom, herself in his. She remembered how she had felt standing naked on the cement slab, before the weight had lifted.

Bee nodded. "Yeah," she said, "I know."

Finally their mother stopped talking, and then Jacky said, "I'm done," and put his napkin next to his plate, still mounded with ribs, and got up and left. He walked through the living room and out the front door and Bee and her mother and father sat at the table and listened to the door close and the sound of him leaving in the car.

Bee kept breathing, in and out, especially *out*. After a while she settled into where she was: there, in an awful moment, with her parents. There.

They tried to eat. Bee wanted to look at her father, but couldn't, yet. She looked at her mother, who raised her eyebrows and managed a shaky I'm-not-crying smile. It made Bee want to touch her. A few seconds later she leaned a little forward, toward her mother, and said to her, "The ribs are good, Mom."

They cleared the dishes as if they had finished their

dinner, and then Bee's mother said, "Oh, let's just leave them for now," and didn't even bother to wipe the counters or sweep the floor. Bee's father disappeared into the garage; Bee and her mother went and sat in front of the TV and after a while her mother fell asleep, an open *Time* magazine in her lap.

Jacky was still gone. His news sat inside Bee, but it wasn't a brick, like before. It was what he was going to do, his way out. And there *wasn't* a huge war going on—the more she thought about it, she was pretty sure of that. She rested her head against the back of her chair. She knew her father was sitting in the garage, retreated inside himself, on the other side of the wall from where she was in the family room. She remembered how he had come around to talk to her after she had fainted.

She got up, opened the door from the family room into the garage, and found him where she knew he would be. He wasn't doing anything, just sitting on the old couch, looking at his hands.

"Hi," he said, as if she had caught him at something.

"Hi," Bee answered. She had a momentary impulse to step back inside and leave him to himself.

But her father spoke. "Whatcha up to?"

Bee shrugged. "Nothing," she said.

"Want to sit?" he asked.

She did want to. She stepped off the threshold—a skip, almost—and walked over to the couch and sat down in the middle of the middle cushion, close to but not touching her father. The plaid upholstery was a little scratchy against the backs of her thighs, and she put her hands underneath them and let her legs swing back and forth. Neither she nor her father said anything. It was cool in the garage, and she liked how the light was dim and soft.

She asked him, "Why did you faint?" It wasn't even that hard just to go ahead and ask what she wanted to know.

Her father kept looking at his hands. "Oh," he said. "We found some of our guys on crosses. We cut them down, brought all the bodies together. After that—that's when I fainted."

Bee saw her father rescuing men off crosses, even though they were already dead; she saw him carrying the wounded, before he was one of them. She thought about how people saved or were saved. And she saw that sometimes when they thought that was what they were doing, they weren't saving or being saved at all.

Her father exhaled. He looked as if he were learning to whistle, raising up his eyebrows, blowing out air. Then he said to Bee, "Why did you? Faint?"

"I don't know," Bee told him. She didn't have

anything to compare with guys on crosses. "The bull?" she said. But she knew that wasn't it. Whatever it was had been *inside* her, and so heavy that it finally made her fall down, just like the burning was inside her, and the light. She just didn't have words for it, and then she was glad that words weren't so important with her father.

"Well, *here* you two are." Bee's mother had opened the family room door into the garage and was standing there, her hand resting on her hip. "I wondered where everyone disappeared to."

Bee and her father smiled.

"What would you say to a hot fudge sundae?" she asked. "I have all the makings, and the more I think about it, this is a big step for Jacky, a *big* step, and we should make the most of it. We should celebrate."

Bee looked at her mother standing in the doorway, talking the way she always talked about things that scared her. "Sure," Bee said. She loved hot fudge sundaes.

"All right, then," her mother said. "I'll get started."

Bee and her father stood up off the couch and her father awkwardly patted the top of her shoulder. "OK, Prize," he said. "It's OK."

"Yeah," Bee answered, nodding, and then, "Hot fudge," and they went into the kitchen, to make the sundaes and to wait for Jacky to come home.

Carolyn Coman "has a generous, inclusive vision of what it means to be sane," wrote the *Village Voice* in its review of her first novel, *Tell Me Everything*. Her second book, *What Jamie Saw*, was a National Book Award finalist and a Newbery Honor Book.

Carolyn Coman lives in South Hampton, New Hampshire. She has a daughter and a son.